THE PUPPY PLACE

BARKLEY

THE PUPPY PLACE

BARKLEY

ELLEN MILES

SCHOLASTIC INC.

For Lauren and the herd

Copyright © 2023 by Ellen Miles
Cover art by Tim O'Brien
Original cover design by Steve Scott

ISBN 978-1-338-84733-8

10 9 8 7 6 5 4 3 2 1   23 24 25 26 27

Printed in the U.S.A.   40
First printing 2023

CHAPTER ONE

"Over here, Buddy!" Lizzie clapped her hands and watched, smiling, as her little brown puppy looked up, spotted her, and dashed toward her, leaving behind a cluster of other dogs in all different sizes and shapes.

"What a good boy," Lizzie said as Buddy sat panting in front of her. She popped a liver treat into his mouth and he gobbled it down, wagging his tail. Then he grinned up at her and wagged his tail even harder. You didn't have to be able to speak Dog to know what he was saying.

"You want more treats?" Lizzie asked. She laughed. "Maybe later. Go on and play." She waved him away, and Buddy zipped off to meet up with another bunch of dogs, over by the wading pool. Lizzie shook her head as she watched him go. Buddy really was such a good dog. Even here at the dog park, with so many wonderful distractions, he came to her when she called.

Lizzie loved the dog park almost as much as Buddy did. She loved watching all the different dogs play together. There were big ones and small ones, shy dogs and outgoing pups—and they all seemed to get along. Their owners were interesting, too. There were young couples, older people, and sometimes a mom or dad who was juggling kids and dogs, running from the playground to the dog park and back again.

Why didn't she come more often? Lizzie usually only went to the dog park when she had a foster puppy who needed some extra socialization—that is, a puppy who needed to learn how to get along with other dogs and people.

Lizzie's family, the Petersons, were a foster family for puppies who needed homes. They took each one in just for a little while, until they could find the perfect home for that puppy. Every puppy was different, and Lizzie loved getting to know them and figuring out what type of home would be best.

With most puppies, it was enough to stay home and play with Buddy in the Petersons' fenced yard. Buddy had started out as a foster puppy, but he'd ended up being a permanent part of the family. Now, along with Lizzie's younger brothers, Charles and the Bean, Buddy helped each new foster puppy feel at home. He was always friendly and welcoming, always ready to share his toys, his treats, and his family.

But it had been a little while since their last foster puppy, and Lizzie had started to wonder if Buddy was feeling a bit bored and lonely. The dog park was the perfect solution. He could run and play and meet new dogs—without even having to share his toys!

Now Buddy was zooming around in circles, chasing and being chased—two of his favorite things to do. In front of Buddy was a tiny, fluffy, rust-colored Pomeranian, yapping his head off as he scampered along. Behind Buddy was a big, galumphing golden retriever who wagged her feathery tail as she ran, letting out deep woof-woofs, as if yelling "Wait for me, wait for me!"

Soon, some other dogs joined the fun: Lizzie spotted a sleek gray Weimaraner and a curly-haired Airedale mix. (Lizzie could identify the breed of pretty much any dog she saw, since she was always studying the Dog Breeds of the

World poster on her bedroom wall.) Then she saw a pair of brown-and-white spaniels that looked very familiar. "Zig! Zag!" Lizzie yelled when she saw them. They had been two of her favorite foster pups, even if they had been quite a handful. The hardest part had been telling them apart since they were practically twins. Their coloring was exactly the same, with each brown spot in the same place on each pup. Lizzie headed over to talk to their owner. She didn't always get a chance to see her foster puppies once they were adopted. She couldn't wait to hear how they were doing.

"Hey, Lizzie!"

Lizzie turned—and groaned. Her best friend, Maria, was running toward her across the dog park.

Lizzie loved Maria, she really did. But she knew why Maria was here.

"Your mom told me you were here. I thought we were going to get together after dog-walking, to talk about the sleepover!" Maria said breathlessly as she approached.

Lizzie, Maria, and two other friends had a dog-walking business. Every day after school, they walked dogs for people who needed a little help with their pets. Lizzie usually did some training as well, since she loved helping dogs learn how to be their best selves. She was always happy to help when a client begged her to teach a dog to stop barking, or come when called.

She and Maria had both done their dog-walking routes that day, but then Lizzie had "forgotten" that they'd made plans to meet. "Oh, right," she said now. "Sure." Maria was really excited about a sleepover party she was planning, and Lizzie—wasn't. Why? Because it was going to be a Spooky Sleepover, where everyone told their scariest stories.

Scary stories were very popular lately in Lizzie's grade. Everyone talked about the horror movies they'd watched over the weekend, or the Goosebumps books they were reading.

Lizzie didn't watch horror movies.

She didn't read scary stories.

She did not see the point. Wasn't being scared a bad thing? It was for her. If she heard a scary story it stuck with her forever, keeping her awake at night. Why did people think it was fun to be scared? She just didn't get it—but so far, she had not shared these feelings with Maria. She didn't want her best friend to think she was a chicken, or a baby.

"Yeah, great!" Lizzie pasted on a big smile, pretending to be excited about the party. "I'm so glad you found me. So tell me what you're thinking."

Maria started to talk about skeleton decorations—"Like a family of skeletons, maybe even a dog skeleton, maybe the kind that move!" she said—and about scary snacks, like hot dogs made to look like bloody fingers.

Lizzie nodded and smiled. She didn't even want to think about bloody fingers, much less eat them. Ew. But she pretended to be into all of it. "Cool," she said, and "Ooh, scary!" She felt as if the sleepover was a monster that was walking slowly toward her. She just wanted to run away— but how could she let Maria down?

"Whoa, watch out!" Maria said suddenly.

But it was too late. Out of nowhere, something huge banged hard into Lizzie. A monster? Lizzie turned as she tried to find her balance. She saw shaggy white fur and a wide-open mouth, all sharp teeth and pink tongue.

But it wasn't a monster.

It was a dog.

CHAPTER TWO

"Oof," said Lizzie, as she landed—hard—on her butt. She'd teetered and tottered for a moment, but in the end she couldn't keep herself upright. Now she gasped, catching her breath as she rubbed her right elbow, which she'd banged on the ground as she fell.

The dog loomed over her, his mouth still hanging open in—yikes, was that a snarl, or a smile?

Lizzie decided to see it as a smile. "Hey, there," she said weakly as she reached up a hand to let him sniff her scent. She knew it was always best to let a dog get to know you before you started petting him.

He snuffled her hand for two seconds, then came in fast for some huge, slobbery kisses, licking Lizzie's face thoroughly until every inch of it was damp.

"Don't be scared!" called out a woman's voice. "He's friendly!"

"Um, yeah," said Lizzie under her breath. "Kinda got that feeling." This was one of her aunt Amanda's pet peeves: owners who let their dogs run wild, jumping all over people, while they called out, "He's friendly!"—as if that made it all okay.

She tried to push the dog away a little so she could get up, but the big white pup was so huge and heavy. And he wouldn't stop licking her! "Maria!" Lizzie cried. "Help!"

"I'll get him," called that voice again. "Barkley, you naughty boy! Stop that right now."

The dog ignored her.

"Barkley!" the woman said, a little more sternly. "No!"

Barkley put his big, heavy paws on Lizzie's shoulders and leaned against her in a furry, warm hug. He snuffled in her ear as if he was telling her a secret, wagging his long, feathery tail.

Don't mind her. I never do! She gives me treats anyway.

Maria had grabbed Lizzie's wrist, and now she pulled Lizzie up and away from the big, shaggy white dog. Lizzie stumbled to her feet and began to brush herself off. Dog hair, mud—it was nothing new for Lizzie, really. The mess didn't bother her.

The badly trained dog did.

A small, red-faced woman reached down and grabbed the dog's collar. "How many times have I told you, you silly boy?" she said, but she couldn't keep the smile out of her voice. She turned to Lizzie. "Sorry," she said. "Are you okay?"

Lizzie nodded. "I'm fine," she said.

"I know Barkley looks like a full-grown dog, but he's just a puppy. He's not even a year old," said the woman.

"A Great Pyrenees," said Lizzie, nodding. "Looks like he already weighs a hundred pounds or more. He'll be even bigger when he's a bit older." She bit her lip. She really wanted to add, "That's why it's so important to train him now," as her aunt Amanda would have, but she didn't want to make the owner mad. Lizzie had found out that grown-ups didn't always like it when a kid offered training advice, even if the kid happened to know more about dogs than most adults. At least, that's what Aunt Amanda always said about Lizzie.

"Wow, good call!" said the woman. "Not many people are familiar with this breed. You must know a lot about dogs."

"She knows *so* much," said Maria. "Like, everything." She ticked off topics on her fingers. "Dog breeds, dog nutrition, dog grooming, dog training . . ."

"Maybe I could help, um—" Lizzie began. What was the best approach?

"Oh, thanks, but there's no need," said the woman, waving a hand. "I know he needs to learn some manners. I've been watching some videos and I've got some things to try."

Lizzie winced. She knew that there were a lot of dog trainers online. A few of them really knew what they were doing, but a lot of them didn't.

Aunt Amanda had helped her understand the difference.

"Great," said Lizzie. By now, Barkley had charged off to play with—or anyway jump on top of—a poodle that had passed by, and Buddy had circled back around to check in with Lizzie. "If you ever want some local help, you can give Bowser's Backyard a try," Lizzie said as she petted Buddy. "There are some very good trainers there." That was her aunt Amanda's doggy day-care business.

"Mmm, can't afford that," said the woman, shrugging. "I can barely afford to feed that big lug." She pointed to Barkley, who was at that moment stealing a rope tug toy from a boxer.

"Or you could just call Lizzie," said Maria. "She and her family foster puppies, and they are great with dogs." She scribbled down Lizzie's name and number on a scrap of paper she pulled from her backpack.

The woman took it and shoved it in her pocket. She turned around, looking for her puppy. "Barkley?" she yelled. "Where are you?"

Lizzie pointed to a corner of the dog park, where Barkley and three other dogs were rolling in a mud puddle.

"Argh!" said the woman, throwing up her hands. "Barkley!" She strode off to grab him, without saying goodbye.

Lizzie and Maria looked at each other, shrugged, and laughed.

"You're like my public relations person," said Lizzie, linking arms with her best friend as they left the dog park with Buddy. "You made me sound like a professional dog trainer."

"Well, you kind of are," said Maria. "That lady needs some help with that dog, for sure. It's too bad she wasn't going to listen to you." She grinned at Lizzie. "Now, about that sleepover," she said.

"C'mon, I'll walk you home and we can talk about it."

Lizzie groaned inwardly but put on a happy face as Maria chatted about setting up the family room with spooky lighting. "Maybe we could make a tape with some scary sound effects," she said. "Like 'oooooooOOOOOOOOOoooo' and 'eeeeeekkkk!'"

Lizzie felt the hair on the back of her neck stand up, even though she knew the ghostly noises were coming straight from her friend's mouth. "Sure, fun!" she said. "I bet Charles and Sammy would love to help." Her brother and his best friend were always up for goofing around with stuff like that.

Maria grinned. "Great idea," she said, giving Lizzie a quick hug. "I'm so glad we decided to do this. I can't think of anyone I'd rather co-host with."

Lizzie had a flash of the tea parties she used to host for all her stuffed dogs, back when she was little. Now, that was fun. Pretending to drink tea and munch on tiny sandwiches? What was better than that? But those days were past, and now it was skeletons and screaming.

Just as they started to walk up the Petersons' porch stairs, Lizzie heard a car honking behind them. "Hey!" called a familiar voice. "I think you were right. I do need help with Barkley."

CHAPTER THREE

Lizzie stared at the woman, who had pulled over and was climbing out of her car. "Wait, how did you find me?" she asked.

The woman shrugged. "Everybody at the dog park seemed to know about the Petersons and how great they are with puppies. You're famous." She looked down at her feet. "Actually, Barkley knocked over another little girl just after you left. That's when I started to think that maybe I should take you up on your offer."

Another little girl? Lizzie put her hands on her hips, ready to tell this lady off. She was no "little girl." But Maria touched her arm and gave her a look that made her stop before she started.

Just then, Lizzie's mom opened the front door. Buddy dashed inside, probably running to get one of his favorite toys to show to Barkley. "Hello?" Mom said to the woman, who was now striding right up the walk, with Barkley straining at his leash in front of her. "Can I help you with something?"

The woman laughed. "I sure hope so. This is Barkley, and I'm Sonia. Your daughter and her friend were very convincing about being able to help me teach him some manners."

Mom raised her eyebrows. "Well . . ." she began, "we're not exactly in the training business."

"Just a few days," said Sonia. "That's all I'm asking for. I have to go on a business trip tomorrow, and I was going to have a dog-sitter come to my apartment, but I wasn't feeling great about that. Now these girls have talked me into letting you take care of him for a while—and hopefully he'll be easier to deal with by the time I get back."

Mom looked at Lizzie and raised an eyebrow. Lizzie gave her head the tiniest shake, just to let Mom know that this was not exactly what had happened. She'd never offered to board and train Barkley!

Lizzie looked down at the big white pup, who was now sitting nicely next to Sonia as if on his best behavior. He gazed back at Lizzie with shiny black eyes. He twitched his ears into a "please?" sort of look and thumped his big tail on the ground.

Can I come visit for a while? I'd love to get to know you.

He was so handsome, with his big, noble head, his lovely warm brown eyes, his long feathered white coat, and his huge chunky paws. His black nose made him look a little like a polar bear, right there on her very own front porch. A polar bear that Lizzie was longing to cuddle with.

"I do think we could help him," Lizzie said. She put on her own pleading look, the one that Mom usually had a hard time resisting. "It's short-term, anyway. And we haven't had a foster puppy in a while."

Mom sighed and threw up her hands. She knew when to give in. "Fine," she said. "As long as you and your brother take care of him. I should check with your dad, but—" She shrugged, and Lizzie smiled. They all knew it would be okay with Dad. Puppies were always okay with Dad.

Lizzie and Maria grinned at each other and did a little fist bump.

"I'd better head home," said Maria. "I'll see you tomorrow, okay, Barkley?" She knelt down to give the big dog a hug, and then she was off.

"Come on, Barkley," said Lizzie. "Let's get you settled in." She left the grown-ups to figure out the details as she headed inside with Barkley. He sat calmly while she unclipped his leash, then began to follow Lizzie around the house, sniffing and checking things out. Already, he seemed more mellow, less wild. He was curious, Lizzie could see that, but somehow he seemed—respectful? Like a polite guest.

"You're a good boy at heart, I can see that," said Lizzie, as they entered the kitchen. "Oops! No, Barkley!"

The polite guest had gone straight to Buddy's bowl and scarfed up the few remaining kibbles from Buddy's breakfast. Buddy usually liked to save those for a late-afternoon snack.

Barkley sat down and looked at her with his head cocked.

Sorry! Did I do something wrong?

"It's okay," said Lizzie. "I guess you're hungry, huh? We'll get you set up with your own bowl for dinnertime."

Buddy, who had followed them into the kitchen, didn't seem bothered. He just scratched at the back door as if suggesting that they all go outside to play.

"Good idea, Bud," said Lizzie. She already knew that Buddy and Barkley would be fine together since they'd run around a bit at the dog park. She opened the door and the dogs ran out into the Petersons' fenced backyard.

She sat on the back deck and watched them play. This was one of the best parts about being a foster family. Buddy loved meeting all the new puppies, and it was always interesting to see how he interacted with each one. Lizzie noticed that Barkley was gentle with the smaller pup; he didn't use his size to intimidate or bully Buddy. He shared toys well and didn't bark as he and Buddy chased each other around and around. Those were all good signs.

"Well," said Mom, coming out the back door. "That was interesting. Somehow I have the feeling that we might end up looking for a new home for Barkley. I think even if he's better trained he might just be too much dog for Sonia." She sat with Lizzie and watched the dogs run. "He seems like a sweetheart, though." After a few minutes, she stood up. "I'm off to pick up the Bean at day care. Your dad will be home in a couple minutes. I've called him to tell him about Barkley coming to stay for a while and—surprise!—he's okay with it."

By bedtime that night, Barkley seemed to feel totally at home. He had been sweet and gentle with the Bean, and he'd let Charles and Lizzie brush his beautiful long coat. He'd also eaten three bowls of dog food. "Hmm," Dad had said, watching the big pup scarf down the kibble. "Large as you are, I guess you're still a growing boy, Barkley." He'd promised to pick up an extra-large bag of dog food on his way home from work the next day.

Lizzie brought Barkley into her room to sleep. She made him his own bed on the floor since he seemed way too big to share hers. He curled up on it, but when Lizzie turned off her light, he got up and paced around, whining at the door. "What?" she asked. "You don't like being cooped up in here?" She decided it was okay to let him out of her bedroom; he was definitely house-trained and he did not seem to be a chewer. She heard the big pup pad down the hall, stopping at each bedroom door in turn as if he was checking up on the family. Then she heard him thump down on the rug by the top of the stairs. "Sleep tight, Barkley!" she called. But she had a feeling he would be wakeful through the night, keeping an eye on them all.

CHAPTER FOUR

"Be a good boy, Barkley," said Lizzie as she gave him one last pat before leaving for school the next morning. He rolled over on his back with his paws in the air, grinning happily at her.

How about a belly rub for a good boy?

Lizzie giggled as she patted his belly. "You're just a giant marshmallow, aren't you?" she said. "You look so huge and scary, but you're a softie inside." She stood up reluctantly, hating to leave him. It was never easy to leave for school when they had a new foster puppy in the house.

"I'll take good care of him, I promise," said Mom. "But come home right after school. I have an interview to do this afternoon and I really can't be late since I've already rescheduled it twice. You'll need to be here for Barkley."

Lizzie's mom was a newspaper reporter, and she was always working on something interesting. "I will," said Lizzie. "Barkley can come with me on my dog-walking route. I think he'll get along just fine with all my clients." She gave Barkley one more pet, then stood up and grabbed her backpack.

Lizzie thought about Barkley all day at school. What would be the best way to train him not to jump up? What other types of training did he need? He seemed pretty mellow when he was at the Petersons'—was it something about Sonia that made him act out when he was around her? Aunt Amanda always said that most dog behavior problems had more to do with the people than with the dog.

At lunchtime, Lizzie went to the media center to do a little research on Great Pyrenees. By the time the last bell rang, she couldn't wait to get home to Barkley.

But when she and Maria walked out of school, Lizzie saw Mom waving from the window of their van. "Lizzie! You're going to have to come with us." Lizzie ran over, Maria right behind her.

"What happened?" Lizzie said. "Is Barkley okay?" She saw the big white dog lying in the way-back, very still. In the middle seat, the Bean sat buckled into his car seat.

"Barkley is fine," said Mom. "But the Bean has the sniffles, so they sent him home from day care. I absolutely have to get to this interview, so you'll have to come with me so you can watch the Bean while I work. I brought Barkley along, too, just because I didn't know how he'd behave if he was alone in the house."

"I can cover your dog-walking clients," Maria offered as Lizzie climbed into the van.

"Oh, thank you, Maria," said Mom. "That would be wonderful. Buckle up, Lizzie!" They drove off before Lizzie could say another thing.

"Where are we going?" Lizzie asked. She reached over to pick up a juice box that the Bean had dropped between them on the seat, and gave it back to him. His nose was runny, but otherwise he looked fine.

"To a farm," Mom said. "I'm profiling a couple who are homesteading out near the state park."

"What's homesteading?" asked Lizzie as she reached back to pet Barkley.

"Basically, it's people who are trying to live without buying much, or anything," Mom explained. "They grow their own vegetables, have a cow for milk, and try to be as self-sufficient as possible. Like, if they need to fix the plumbing they figure out how to do it themselves rather than call a plumber."

"Cool," said Lizzie.

"These folks also have sheep, goats, and chickens," said Mom. "And I think a horse or two."

"Maybe they'd like a dog, too," Lizzie said. "Barkley would probably love living on a farm."

"Well, he's not really ours to give away, remember?" Mom asked. "For now, we're just keeping him for a week, then he goes back to Sonia."

We'll see about that, thought Lizzie. She had a feeling that Sonia and Barkley were not the best match. In her opinion, Sonia would do better with a small dog that was easier to control and more comfortable in her apartment.

"Was Barkley a good boy today?" Lizzie asked.

Mom nodded. "He basically slept all day."

"Oh! That makes perfect sense," said Lizzie. "Because guess what I read today? Great Pyrenees are nocturnal!"

"What, like bats or raccoons?" Mom asked. "They're only active at night?"

"Well, of course they have adjusted to daytime life over time," said Lizzie. "But they were first used as guard dogs, so it made sense that they liked to stay up all night. I have a feeling that Barkley was watching over us while we were sleeping last night."

"Interesting. As long as he's not chewing things up or making messes, I guess it doesn't matter," said Mom as she drove down a long dirt driveway.

"Villa Villekula Farm," Lizzie read off the sign on the big red barn. "That's the name of Pippi Longstocking's house!" She loved those books about the brave, independent girl with red pigtails.

Mom laughed. "I can see where they got the name," she said, waving back to a young woman who was welcoming them to the farm. The woman had bright red hair, tied in two long braids. She wore faded overalls, a plaid shirt, and knee-high green boots that were covered in mud—and she was actually holding a pitchfork! Lizzie thought she looked like an illustration in a picture book about a farmer.

"That's Lauren," Mom said quickly to Lizzie. "Our interview should only take about half an hour. Please help me out and wait in the car with the Bean and Barkley."

Lizzie was disappointed. She thought that Lauren looked like an interesting person, and the farm seemed like a cool place. There was a big white house and the red barn, and lots of smaller sheds and shelters dotted the yard. She spotted a fenced-in corral out back, where two white horses grazed under a huge, spreading tree. A smaller fenced-in area in the front yard held a dozen or so goats with floppy ears.

"What if I take Barkley and the Bean for a walk?" Lizzie asked. "So we don't have to be cooped up in the car."

Mom was already rushing off, notebook in hand, to meet Lauren. "If you're sure you can handle both of them," she called back.

Of course, Lizzie was sure.

Until Barkley jumped out of the car before she'd clipped on his leash.

CHAPTER FIVE

"No, Barkley!" Lizzie yelled. But it was too late. The big white pup was already charging straight for Mom and Lauren. She knew exactly what he was going to do: Barkley was going to jump up on Lauren and knock her down.

But he surprised Lizzie.

He ran right past the red-headed farmer.

"Barkley!" Lizzie yelled again when she saw where he was heading. "No! Leave the chickens alone!" She grabbed the Bean's hand. "Come on," she told her little brother. "Run! We have to stop Barkley before he—"

"Before he what?" the Bean asked, wide-eyed.

Lizzie shook her head. She didn't even want to think about what could happen if Barkley got into the chickens.

"Yo! Dog!" yelled Lauren. "Stop! Hey!" She ran after Barkley, too. He was headed straight for the chicken coop, where dozens of chickens scratched in the dirt in their fenced area.

The chickens saw him coming. They clucked and flapped their wings and ran this way and that. Feathers flew as they kicked up dust in their hurry to run from the dog.

Lizzie knew that Buddy would never have been able to resist jumping over that low fence and chasing the chickens. When he saw something running that way, Buddy's instinct was to run after it. He loved to chase squirrels so much that the Petersons didn't even say the word out loud anymore. If he even heard anyone start to say "squ," he went wild, running around the house as if he was searching for a fluffy gray rodent. (The Petersons' code word was "gray thing" if they wanted to talk about squirrels at the bird feeder.)

But Barkley was different, it turned out. Instead of jumping into their pen, Barkley stopped short at the fence, lay down, and calmly watched the chickens do their wacky chicken thing.

"I'm so sorry," Mom was saying to Lauren as Lizzie approached, the Bean in tow. "I can't apologize enough. Really, I—"

"It's okay," Lauren said, holding up a hand. "I thought that was going to be a disaster, but we got lucky."

"I'm Lizzie," said Lizzie. "I'll get him out of here." She held up the leash in her hand.

"Probably a good idea before he sees the goats," Lauren said, smiling.

Lizzie couldn't believe how calm Lauren was. She had what Lizzie's dad would call "a good head on her shoulders." She didn't get all squawky like the chickens. Maybe you had to be that way, to be a homesteader. Lizzie clipped on Barkley's leash and led him away, taking the Bean with her. "We'll walk down the driveway," she called to Mom as she headed off.

"You're a naughty dog," Lizzie said to Barkley. "But, well, you're a good dog, too." He looked up at her with his intelligent brown eyes and wagged his feathery tail.

I just wanted to see everything. What a cool place!

Lizzie and Barkley and the Bean walked slowly up and down the driveway four times before Mom came driving up in the van, finished with her interview.

"I'm sorry, Mom," Lizzie said right away. "He just jumped out before I could stop him."

"It's okay," Mom said. She buckled the Bean into his car seat while Lizzie got Barkley settled in the way-back. "Thankfully Lauren seemed to take it in stride. We had a great conversation. She and her husband, Erik, are really working hard to create a life that feels right to them."

"Cool," said Lizzie as Mom drove back down the long and winding driveway. "I wonder if it would feel right to them to adopt an amazing dog. Did you see how calm Barkley was around those chickens?"

"I did," said Mom. "And I know Lauren did, too. And as a matter of fact, I asked her if they might be interested in adopting Barkley—that is, if Sonia decides to give him up."

"Really?" Lizzie leaned forward. This was

exciting news. She thought that Villa Villekula farm would be the perfect spot for a dog like Barkley. "What did she say?"

Mom shook her head sadly. "She loves dogs, and she thought Barkley was great, but she said that she and Erik are just getting by, and they can't afford another mouth to feed. Especially a mouth attached to a really huge, growing dog!"

Lizzie sat back in her seat, shoulders slumping. She hated to think about Barkley going back to live all cooped up in a tiny apartment with Sonia. He was a big boy with lots of energy, and he needed lots of space where he could run and play.

And it wasn't only about the apartment. Sonia was nice, and she meant well, but Lizzie could see that she really did not have the right personality to deal with a big dog like Barkley. Lizzie had a feeling that Sonia knew it, too.

Back at home, Lizzie took Buddy and Barkley out

back to play. Maria stopped by after she finished seeing to all her and Lizzie's dog-walking clients, and Lizzie told her about Lauren and her cool farm.

Barkley came over for some attention, and Maria threw her arms around him. "How could anybody say no to this guy?" The shaggy white pup leaned in to the hug, nuzzling Maria's cheek.

Nobody ever really has!

Maria giggled. "He's such a sweetie," she said.

"He's smart, too," said Lizzie. "I pretty much taught him how to stop pulling on the leash, just during the time Mom was interviewing Lauren." She scritched Barkley between the ears. "He's very mature for a dog this young. He's kind of an old soul."

Barkley gazed into Lizzie's eyes and she felt her heart melt. "You really are special," she told him.

"So about the party," Maria said. "My dad and I went over the list of movies we might watch. They're scary but not too gory or anything. Dad says we're too young for the really bloody stuff. He thinks we're babies or something."

Lizzie felt like putting her hand up. *Baby? Yup, that's me!* But she just nodded. "Great," she said. She hugged Barkley close, wishing she could bring him to the party. There was something about him that made her feel so safe and protected. But truthfully, she didn't want to watch scary movies, even with Barkley at her side.

CHAPTER SIX

"And they're planning to get some more animals next spring, maybe sheep or even an alpaca," Mom said. She passed the mashed potatoes to Lizzie. It was dinnertime, and Mom was telling everyone about her interview with Lauren. "I just think it's so cool what they're trying to do," her mom continued. "I mean, not too many people would be into it, but just think! No supermarket, no big box stores— they don't even have a heating bill because they heat with a woodstove and cut all their wood from their land." She shook her head. "Amazing. They're even growing their own wheat to bake their bread with."

"Maybe you secretly want to be a pioneer

woman," Dad said. "Should we get a goat or two for the backyard?"

He was teasing, but Mom looked interested. "As a matter of fact, it turns out that goats are really cute and smart," she said. "They're almost like dogs. You wouldn't believe how affectionate they are with Lauren. All they want is to be petted and get treats, just like Buddy. They even have great names: Potato, Mouse, Shirley . . ."

"Well, it sounds like it'll be an excellent article," Dad said, helping himself to another piece of meat loaf.

Lizzie dragged her fork through the ketchup left on her plate. "May I be excused?" she asked.

Mom's eyebrows rose. "Aren't you hungry? You usually have seconds or even thirds on mashed potatoes."

"I guess I'm just tired," Lizzie said. "And I have some homework to do." Really, she just wanted to lie on her bed, cuddle with Barkley, and forget all about Maria's party.

"Sure," said Mom. "Put your plate in the dishwasher and grab a couple of cookies for dessert. Lauren gave me some amazing oatmeal-date bars that she baked just for us."

Lizzie cleared her plate, took two cookies, and headed upstairs with Barkley following on her heels. She lay down and patted the bed. "Come on, hang with me," she told the big pup. He leapt up and snuggled next to her, taking up most of the bed. Lizzie giggled as he snuffled at her cheek, and Barkley thumped his tail.

I love being cozy with you.

Lizzie nibbled at her cookies and scratched Barkley between the ears. It was nice to just be quiet together. His big, warm body made her feel calm, somehow. She petted him for a while, then picked up her book and read a chapter out loud to him. Barkley seemed to enjoy it.

"Knock, knock?" Dad was standing in her door-way. "You okay, sweet pea? You were awfully quiet at dinner."

Lizzie shrugged. "I'm fine," she said.

Dad sat down on the very edge of her bed, the only space left. "Really?" he asked. "Because I get the feeling that something's bothering you."

Lizzie sighed. "It's nothing. It's just—this party that Maria's having on Saturday. It's got a whole, like, horror theme. Scary decorations and scary music and scary stories and scary movies. She's so excited about it, but I'm—"

"Not," Dad finished for her. "Yeah, that's not really your cup of tea, is it? It's not for me, either. Your mom loves that stuff, but I never really got the appeal."

Lizzie smiled at him. "Maybe I could just tell her I'm sick or something," she said. That was the only plan she'd come up with so far to avoid the party. She didn't like to lie to her best friend, but maybe if she was lucky she'd have a cold by the weekend and then it wouldn't be a lie.

"Or maybe you could just tell her the truth," suggested Dad.

Lizzie shook her head. "It's too embarrassing," she said. "Everybody else in our class loves scary stuff. I'm the only baby."

"You might be wrong about that," he said. "But even if you're not, don't you think Maria would understand?"

Lizzie dug her fingers into the soft, thick fur at Barkley's neck. "Maybe," she said. "Or maybe she'd laugh at me."

"Did I laugh at you when you told me you were scared about the monster under your bed or about the burglars in the closet?" Dad asked.

"No," Lizzie said, in a small voice. Dad had always been great about helping her when she was scared. When she was little and worried about monsters under the bed, he hadn't laughed. Instead, he'd helped her make a special monster-repelling device (actually it was a shoebox they'd glued knobs and dials onto). "But you're my dad and you love me."

"Well, Maria's your best friend, and she loves you, too," Dad said. "I think you should trust that." He ruffled Lizzie's hair. "Teeth all brushed?" he asked. "Ready to be tucked in?"

She nodded.

Dad pulled the blankets up around Lizzie's chin and gave her a kiss. "Sweet dreams," he said. "Looks like you've got some good company tonight as long as he doesn't take over the whole bed."

Lizzie smiled at Barkley, who lay with his big,

heavy head on her shoulder. "I could never be scared with him around," she said.

She fell asleep with Barkley's soft breath in her ear. She woke later, sometime in the middle of the night, and patted the bed next to her. Barkley had left. When she listened, she could hear him padding down the hall, checking on the Bean, checking on Charles, checking on her parents. Barkley was keeping watch over all of them. She pulled the covers up again, turned over, and went back to sleep.

CHAPTER SEVEN

"Good boy, Barkley!" Lizzie gave Barkley a treat and patted him on the head. Then she smiled at Buddy. "Well, you're a good boy, too, aren't you?" She gave Buddy a treat, too.

The next afternoon, after she'd done her dog-walking route, and Lizzie went back to the dog park. She'd wanted to give Barkley a chance to really run—he was such a big dog that the Petersons' backyard was like a tiny playpen to him. Plus, she'd been working on his manners, and she wanted to see how well he could behave in a more public place. They'd been there for fifteen minutes, and so far, he had not jumped up on anyone. That was great!

Barkley and Buddy trotted off, shoulder to shoulder, like friends who came to a party together. They had gotten to be good pals already, and Lizzie loved watching them play. Barkley was so gentle with the smaller dog.

Lizzie looked toward the entry gate to the dog park. Where was Maria? Lizzie had asked her to come to the dog park, too. She knew her dad was right: She had to tell her friend the truth and the sooner the better. Lizzie was nervous about it, but it had to be done, and the dog park seemed like a good, neutral place to do it. She would tell Maria that she did not like scary movies. Or scary decorations. Or scary foods. If Maria laughed at her or told her to grow up, then at least Lizzie would have an excuse to skip the party.

Now Buddy and Barkley were taking off in different directions, like friends who had decided it was time to mingle with the other party guests. Buddy romped off to say hello to a boxer while Barkley joined a pack of bigger dogs: a Great Dane, some kind of big lab-shepherd mix, and a poodle with wild curls. Lizzie watched to make sure Barkley was on his best behavior. He really was. He play-bowed and chased and let himself be chased, all in good fun.

"Hey, Lizzie!" Maria called, waving as she approached. "Looks like the guys are having a blast."

Lizzie nodded. "Barkley really is a good boy. He just needed a little more guidance than Sonia was giving him."

"Do you think she'll be able to keep up the training?" Maria asked, folding her arms as they stood watching the dogs play. "I mean, Sonia is going to take him back when she gets home from her trip, right?"

Lizzie shrugged. "That's the plan," she said. "But sometimes I wonder. We'll just have to wait and see how things turn out." She took a deep breath. "So," she began, "there's something I wanted to tell you—"

Just then, Buddy dashed across the field, running as fast as he could as a bigger dog chased after him. "Whoa, Buddy looks a little scared!" said Lizzie. She could see the whites of his eyes, and his ears were flattened back against his head.

"Come on, Buddy!" Lizzie called, kneeling down to open her arms to him. He raced up to her, his tail between his legs. The other dog, a sleek Doberman, was close on his heels. But just as Buddy threw himself into her arms, Lizzie saw a white blur as Barkley came out of nowhere, galloping toward them.

The big white pup stationed himself between Lizzie and the oncoming Doberman. He faced the other dog calmly, letting out a few deep woofs to let him know who was boss.

Back off, bully! Can't you see you're scaring my friend?

Buddy scootched deeper into Lizzie's arms, still frightened, but the Doberman skidded to a halt, then turned and ran off in the opposite direction.

"Whoa," said Maria, watching him go.

"I know," said Lizzie. "That was wild. I don't think the Doberman was going to hurt anybody— he looked like he was just playing. But it was a little too much for Buddy. It's so lucky that Barkley was here to protect his friend!"

Lizzie gave Buddy one more squeeze and then let him down. He stuck close to her as she approached Barkley. "Such a good boy, Barkley," she said, giving him a treat from her pocket. As she patted him and praised him, she felt her racing heart slow down again.

"I think I'd better take these two home," Lizzie said. "Buddy might want to stick to his own yard for a little while."

"Okay. Was there something you wanted to tell me?" Maria asked.

Lizzie waved a hand. "Later," she said. "I'll call you after supper." She did not feel like getting into all that right now.

She didn't feel like it after supper, either. Instead, she lay on her bed with Barkley snuggled up to her on one side and Buddy by her feet. "You two are really pals, aren't you?" she asked. She scritched between Barkley's ears with one hand while she tickled Buddy's chest with her toe.

"What do you think, Buddy? Maybe Barkley could live with us forever." She yawned and rubbed her eyes, feeling sleepy.

Lizzie knew that her parents would never agree to keep Barkley. One permanent dog was enough, especially if she and Charles wanted to keep fostering puppies. But she couldn't help dreaming about it every time she fell in love with a foster puppy. And she fell in love with every one of them.

Lizzie must have drifted off to sleep at some point because the next thing she knew she was wakened by loud barking, out in the hallway.

"What? What?" she said, throwing off her covers. Barkley had left sometime in the night, but Buddy was still there. He jumped off the bed and followed her out of her room.

Her parents and Charles appeared out of their rooms as well. Mom gasped. "Oh, no!" she said. "I must have forgotten to put up the baby gate."

Ever since the Bean had graduated to a big-boy bed, they had made sure to keep the baby gate at the top of the stairs at night so he wouldn't fall down them if he wandered out of his room. But the gate was not in place. Instead, Barkley lay across the top of the stairs, guarding them from the Bean, who sat nearby in his rumpled pajamas, clutching his teddy bear. The big white pup was silent now.

"Good boy, Barkley," said Dad. "I can see that you would never let the Bean get near those stairs."

Lizzie petted Barkley's head. This dog really was one of a kind. He needed a home that was as special as he was.

CHAPTER EIGHT

Lizzie stretched and yawned. It had not been easy to get back to sleep after all the excitement in the middle of the night. Now the morning sun streamed through her windows as the smell of pancakes drifted up from the kitchen. "Yay for Saturday!" Lizzie said out loud. Then she remembered. This Saturday was not like most Saturdays. Yes, she got to sleep late. And yes, Dad was making pancakes. And yes, she had the whole day free.

But.

But it was also the last day before Sonia was due home from her trip. That meant saying goodbye to Barkley. Lizzie didn't think she was ready for that.

Plus, later on it would be time for Maria's party. Lizzie knew for sure that she definitely was not ready for that.

She pulled the covers back up over her head. Maybe she could just stay in bed all day and sleep right through the party. Or—maybe she was starting to feel sick! Lizzie swallowed, to see if her throat was sore. Nope. She took a deep breath, to check if she felt stuffed up. No such luck. No headache, no fever, no aches and pains. Unfortunately, she was totally healthy.

Lizzie heard footsteps padding into her room and pulled the covers back down so she could see who it was. "Barkley!" she said. The big white pup came over to her bed and pushed his head against her hand, looking for some pets. He wagged his long, feathery tail as she scritched him between the ears.

Wake up! It's a beautiful day and I want to spend it with you.

"Of course, you're right," she said. "If I stay in bed, I'll miss your last day with us. Good point." She climbed out of bed and pulled on a pair of joggers and a sweatshirt, then headed downstairs with Barkley on her heels.

"Morning, sunshine!" said Dad when she walked into the kitchen. "Just in time. Everyone else has already eaten, but I saved some for you." He got busy at the stove, and a few minutes later, he put a plate piled with pancakes in front of Lizzie.

"Thanks, Dad," Lizzie said, as she poured syrup over the stack.

"My pleasure." He pulled out a chair to sit at

the kitchen table with her. "So, have you talked to Maria yet? The party's tonight, right?"

Lizzie groaned and pushed her plate away. Suddenly, she'd lost her appetite. She shook her head. "Not yet," she said. "I was going to talk to her, but—you know—stuff happened."

Barkley, sitting at her side, pushed his head against her leg.

Um, if you're not going to eat those—

Lizzie petted Barkley's head. "Has he had breakfast?" she asked. "He seems hungry."

"Three breakfasts by my count," Dad said with a smile. "This dog is going to eat us out of house and home."

"No pancakes for you, then," Lizzie said to Barkley. She took a small bite and remembered how good Dad's pancakes were. Her appetite returned and she dug in. "I'll call Maria right after breakfast," she told Dad.

But after breakfast it seemed more important to take Barkley outside to play with Buddy. And after that, Lizzie remembered that she had wanted to do some more research on Great Pyrenees. Sometimes learning more about a breed helped a lot when she was trying to figure out the best forever home for one of their foster puppies. She knew Sonia hadn't agreed to give him up yet, but she wanted to be prepared. She took Barkley with her up to Mom's study to use the computer.

With Barkley at her feet, Lizzie pored through page after page about the noble white dogs. "Did you know that your family has been companions to royalty?" she asked Barkley. "And that you are known for your especially sensitive hearing?"

Barkley seemed to enjoy listening to all the

information. He rested his big head on her foot and gazed up at her, taking in everything she told him.

"Oh look, this is interesting," said Lizzie, just as the phone rang.

"Lizzie, it's for you!" Dad called from downstairs.

Lizzie felt her stomach knot up. She could guess who it was. "Hello?" she said, when she'd picked up the phone.

"Hey, bestie!" Maria said. She sounded happy and excited. "Are you coming over to help decorate?"

Lizzie hesitated. "Maybe in a while," she said finally. "I'm pretty busy doing some research about Barkley's breed."

"Oh, that reminds me," Maria said. "Mom said it's fine if you'd like to bring him to the sleepover."

"Really?" Lizzie asked. "That would be—fantastic." Picturing Barkley at her side as she sat on the couch watching a scary movie made everything seem much less—scary.

"I thought that would make you happy," Maria said. She paused. "I mean—I know scary stuff isn't your favorite."

"You do?" Lizzie asked. She held the phone away from her ear and stared at it, shocked.

"Of course!" said Maria. "I guess I just thought that if I made it really fun you might start to understand why I like it." She cleared her throat. "Now I'm thinking that was a pretty bad idea. I feel like I haven't been a very good friend."

"No, you're the best friend ever," said Lizzie. "I'm the one who didn't trust you not to laugh at me if I told you I was scared."

"Oh, Lizzie," said Maria. "I would never laugh at you for that. I get it. We all have things that scare us. Remember how I never want to go on the rides on the class trips to Six Flags? You've never made fun of me for that, right?"

Lizzie sat back in Mom's desk chair, feeling a wave of relief wash over her. "Barkley and I will be over as soon as we can," she told Maria. "And I can't wait to tell you what I just learned. I think I may know the perfect home for Barkley—that is, if Sonia agrees."

CHAPTER NINE

"So, where do you want to put old Shaky Bones?" Lizzie asked, holding up a skeleton. Dad had dropped her and Barkley off that afternoon, an hour or so before the other sleepover guests were due to arrive.

She was so happy to be with Maria and to know that her friend truly understood her. And surprisingly, the scary decorations weren't really all that scary once you got used to them. It was just a bunch of plastic stuff from a store. They'd already draped the mailbox in pretend spiderwebs and hung bats from the porch roof. Now, Lizzie shook the skeleton and made it rattle.

Maria laughed. "Hmmm," she said. "How about right here, by the front door? We can prop him up against the railing."

Lizzie told Barkley to sit while she and Maria got the skeleton set in place. "Good boy," she said when they were done. He'd been so patient.

"Let's take Barkley in to meet Simba," suggested Maria. "They can get to know each other before everyone else gets here."

Simba was a big yellow Lab who belonged to Maria's mother, who was blind. He was her guiding eyes dog. He was the smartest, gentlest, sweetest dog Lizzie had ever known, and she knew he and Barkley would get along beautifully.

"Hi, Lizzie," said Maria's mom when they came inside. "Hi, Barkley. I've heard a lot about you." She leaned over to touch him. "My, you're a big boy, aren't you?" she asked. "Welcome. Simba, say hello."

Simba padded over to touch noses with Barkley. The two dogs sniffed each other, wagging their tails.

"Your dad and I were just putting the final touches on the taco bar," Maria's mom said. "The popcorn is popped and the brownies are almost done. I think we're just about ready for company!"

"It smells so good in here," said Lizzie. "Oh, no! Barkley! That's Simba's food." She ran to grab him as he scarfed up food from Simba's bowl. "I'm so sorry," she told Maria's mom. "He's learned a lot this week, but when he sees food it all goes out the window."

"He's a growing boy," said Maria's mom. "Simba was a big eater when he was a puppy, too."

The doorbell rang just then, and Maria ran to welcome their first guests. Within a few minutes, the house was full of noise as six girls chattered and giggled and shrieked. Barkley and Simba got all the attention any dog could want, with lots of hugs and kisses and pets. The taco bar was demolished in moments as the guests dug in, and soon Maria's dad got busy cutting brownies and making sundaes for everyone.

"Movie time!" Maria announced after dinner, leading everyone into the living room. Lizzie hung back, hugging Barkley. Then she felt a hand on her shoulder. "You and Barkley and Brianna can come with me," said Maria's mom. She crooked a finger, and they followed her to the den. "We set up another movie for you two in here," she said. "Have fun!"

Lizzie stared at Brianna. Brianna looked back at her. "You're a scaredy-cat, too?" Lizzie finally asked.

Brianna nodded. "I can't stand horror movies," she confessed. "I don't even like to see the posters for them."

They settled in happily, Barkley between them on the couch. As soon as the movie started, Lizzie let out a cheer. *"Benji!* My favorite."

"Mine, too," said Brianna.

The best thing about the movie was that they'd both already seen it a million times, so they could talk and joke around while it was on. Brianna asked all about Barkley, and Lizzie told her how special he was. "He's amazing," she said. "And you know what I found out today?"

Before Brianna could guess, Maria came in and plopped herself down next to Lizzie. "What?" she asked when Lizzie gave her a questioning look. She waved a hand. "I've seen that scary movie before. I'd rather be in here with you two. And Barkley, of course." She snuggled up to the big white pup, kissing him on the nose. He kissed her back, licking her cheek as he thumped his tail.

I think I like sleepovers!

"Oh, look, it's my favorite scene," said Brianna, pointing to the screen. All three girls watched, mouthing the dialog they knew by heart from seeing the movie so many times.

"Having fun?" Maria leaned over to whisper into Lizzie's ear.

Lizzie nodded. "It's a great party," she said. "Even for scaredy-cats."

"So, what did you want to tell me before, something you learned about the perfect home for Barkley? Maria asked, when the scene was over.

"Get this," said Lizzie. "Great Pyrenees weren't only guard dogs way back in the old days. Lots of people use them now, to watch over goats and sheep and even chickens!"

"You're kidding," said Maria. "So—"

"Yes!" Lizzie said. "He'd be so perfect for Villa Villekula Farm."

"What? Pippi Longstocking needs a dog?" Brianna asked.

They all laughed, and Lizzie filled Brianna in on Lauren's farm. "You can read the story my mom wrote in tomorrow's paper," she said. "And guess what else? When the photographer went out to take pictures at the farm, Lauren was all upset because that morning she had found coyote tracks near the henhouse. She said she absolutely cannot afford to lose any of her animals."

"Barkley to the rescue!" said Maria. "It's a match made in heaven. Barkley would be so happy, living on a farm like that."

"Yup," said Lizzie. "Now all we have to do is convince Lauren. And Sonia, of course."

CHAPTER TEN

In the morning, Maria's guests gathered around the kitchen counter for Mr. Santiago's famous French toast. The other girls looked bleary-eyed, and Daphne admitted that she hadn't slept at all. "I think I was afraid that I'd have nightmares after watching that scary movie," she told Lizzie and Brianna. "Next time I might hang with you guys." She petted Barkley, who was lurking nearby hoping for scraps to magically fall on the floor. Daphne and Brianna both loved dogs as much as Lizzie did; that was why they were part of the dog-walking business.

"I wish I could adopt this dude," she said, scritching Barkley between the ears. "He's fantastic. He's, like, noble! Like a prince on a white horse, only he *is* the white horse."

Barkley leaned against her leg and gave a little huff of pleasure, loving the attention.

I'd love to watch over all of you, and make sure you're always safe.

"He's the best," said Lizzie. "And I think I've figured out the best home for him, too." She told the girls her idea about Barkley going to the farm.

"But what if his owner doesn't agree?" asked Daphne.

Lizzie shrugged. "I'm guessing that she will," she said. "I think she knows that she and Barkley are not a good fit."

When Mr. Santiago dropped her off at home,

Lizzie tossed her rolled-up sleeping bag on the couch and ran to find her mom. "Mom! Where are you?" she yelled as she ran into the kitchen.

"No need to yell," Mom said. She and Dad were still sitting at the kitchen table, sipping coffee.

"How did it go?" Dad asked. "Not too scary?"

"It was fine," Lizzie said. "Mom, listen, I think Lauren really needs to meet Barkley again. And we have to set up a meeting between her and Sonia, too."

Mom smiled. "I'm two steps ahead of you," she said. "Sonia called this morning and said she was back from her trip, but she asked if we could keep Barkley for a few more days because she's"—Mom made quote marks with her fingers—"just so wiped out." She smiled. "I told her about the research you did, and about Lauren and the farm. I suggested we meet there this afternoon."

"And?" Lizzie asked. "What did she say?" She

pushed her fingers into the thick ruff of fur at Barkley's neck, hoping for the best.

"Well, she seemed a little unsure at first," Mom said. "She said she'd paid a breeder a lot of money for Barkley. But I had the feeling that she was tempted by the idea of a great home for him."

"What about Lauren?" Lizzie asked.

"She's tempted, too," said Mom. "She saw more coyote tracks this morning. But she said there's no way she could pay a lot of money for a dog, on top of having to feed him once she has him."

Lizzie sat down with a thump on one of the kitchen chairs. "So we really still don't know if it'll work out," she said. Suddenly, she felt tired. She put her arms on the table and her head on her arms. Dad reached out to rub her back.

"No, but we'll find out soon enough," Mom said. "Why don't you put your stuff away and maybe take a little nap? I know nobody gets much sleep at these parties. I'll wake you in plenty of time to come with me to the farm."

Lizzie didn't feel like a nap, but she went upstairs and lay down on her bed with her arms around Barkley. "You're such a good boy," she said, into his soft fur. "You deserve the best home. And I know you'd love having a job, keeping watch over all those critters."

Before she knew it, Mom was knocking on her door. "You awake, sweetie?" Mom asked.

Lizzie sat up. "I guess I did fall asleep for a bit," she said. "Is it time to go?"

Mom nodded. "Splash some cold water on your face and we'll get going."

A half an hour later, they pulled into Villa Villekula Farm. Sonia was just getting out of her car as Mom parked.

"Barkley!" Sonia said when Lizzie let the big dog out of the back. Sonia held her arms wide and Barkley pulled his leash out of Lizzie's hands as he charged over. She squealed as he jumped up on her and knocked her to the muddy ground.

"Oh, no," said Lizzie, putting her hand over her mouth. Barkley had not jumped up on anyone in days.

"It's okay, it's okay," said Sonia, struggling to her feet as she tried to wipe off the mud. "He's just happy to see me." She sighed. "And I'm happy to see him, too, but . . ."

Just then, Lauren came around the corner of the barn. "Hi," she called, waving. Quickly, Lizzie grabbed Barkley's leash. She didn't want him to jump up on Lauren. But he just sat and looked at Lauren calmly, thumping his tail.

Hi, nice lady. I remember you.

Lauren came over to pet him. "Hi there, Barkley," she said. "You sure are a handsome dude. And a good boy, too." Lizzie could tell that she was a dog lover and that she understood how special Barkley was.

"So," said Mom after she'd introduced the two women.

"So," said Sonia, who was still brushing off mud.

"So," said Lauren. "Listen, I know these dogs make great guard dogs, and I think it's about time we had some help around here, keeping all the animals safe. But I can't afford to pay cash for Barkley."

Sonia started to say something, but Lauren held up a hand. "Here's what Erik and I have been thinking," she said. "How about if we pay you each week in vegetables, and honey, and eggs, and maybe even some maple syrup if we get some made this spring?"

"Wow," said Sonia. "That's very generous. As

a matter of fact, once I thought over this idea I decided it was a really good one. I love Barkley, but I think he'd be a lot happier with a job to do, living in a place like this." She waved a hand around at the farm. "I was going to suggest that I could help pay for Barkley's keep. I've got several big bags of food to give you—they're already in the car—but I would also be happy to cover his food and vet bills for the coming year if that would help."

"So—you're ready to give him up?" Lizzie asked Sonia.

She nodded. "I'll miss him, but I'm grateful to you and your mom for helping me to understand that this would be a better home for him."

"And you're ready to take him?" Lizzie turned to Lauren.

"More than ready," said Lauren. She knelt to put her arms around Barkley. "But what do you think, big guy?"

Barkley leaned in for one of his sloppy wet kisses, and Lauren burst out laughing. "I think that's a yes," she said.

Lizzie grinned at the pair. She had a feeling that they were going to be very, very happy together. She turned to Sonia. "You know, we foster a lot of puppies," she said. "Maybe one of these days we'll take care of one who would be perfect for you."

"I hope so," said Sonia. She looked just a little bit wistful, watching Barkley and Lauren together.

"In the meantime, you can visit him whenever you come to pick up your veggies and eggs," said Lauren. "I'm sure he'll always be happy to see you—and knock you down into the mud."

Everybody laughed. Lizzie went over to give Barkley one last hug. She felt sure that she had helped to find him the very best forever home.

PUPPY TIPS

Some dogs are happiest when they have a job to do. Border collies love to herd sheep (or geese, or children!); Labs love to retrieve; and German shepherds and dogs like Barkley love to take care of others, whether it's a family or a bunch of critters. Does your dog need a job? You can do some research on the breed to find out what kind of activities will make your dog feel useful and fulfilled.

Dear Reader,

As many of you know, I have a special love for big dogs.
It was especially fun to write about Barkley, and imagine
how much fun it would be to curl up with him the way
Lizzie did. My dog, Zipper, isn't as big as Barkley, but I love
cuddling with him. Like Lizzie, I can be a bit of a scaredy-
cat, and it's always nice to feel like Zipper is there to help
me feel safe and secure. I had fun visiting a goat farm
(it's actually called Villa Villekula Farm and it's owned
by a woman named Lauren with red hair!) when I was
researching this book. The goats were so sweet and each
one had its own personality. I did not bring Zipper along
because he definitely would have wanted to chase the
goats!

Yours from the Puppy Place,

Ellen Miles

THE PUPPY PLACE

**For another book about a
big furry sweetheart, try** BOOMER!

"Did you wipe your feet?" Mom frowned as she pointed to Lizzie's sneakers.

Lizzie sighed. "Yes, I wiped my feet. And I'm barely even inside, anyway! I just came back for another load." She held out her arms, and her mom piled them full: a small cooler, a rolled-up sleeping bag, and a pillow. Lizzie staggered back out into the driveway to hand it all over to her dad, who was packing the van.

"I can't wait to set up our campsite!" she said as she passed the sleeping bag to Dad. "I hope it has a good view of the lake." This was going to be a special trip: a three-day weekend with just Dad and Lizzie and her two younger brothers, Charles and the Bean. And Buddy, of course. How could they leave their adorable puppy behind? They were going camping at Crystal Lake, and they were going to hike and fish and make s'mores and play cards. Mom was really missing out. Not that Mom minded, Lizzie knew. She had plans of her own.

It was time for Mom's annual Fab Four reunion, when she got together for a long weekend with three of her best friends from college. Sometimes they met at a spa or a hotel, but this time "the girls" were coming to the Petersons' house. They'd been there once before, when Lizzie was only five or six years old. She didn't remember much about their visit except that Annie had a loud voice, Risa smelled good, and Joy had brought her a present, a horse doll with a beautiful golden coat and a white mane. Lizzie still had that palomino, the only horse among all the dog figurines on her shelf. There had also been a lot of laughter. Lizzie remembered that. The "girls" were always laughing. Risa's laugh was especially memorable: she sounded like a donkey braying, which always made everyone else laugh even more.

Now the girls were about to arrive for a three-day visit. Mom, who didn't normally care so much about people wiping their feet, had been cleaning for weeks. She had bought bright new curtains for the living room, and fluffy new towels, and pretty little soaps that smelled like coconut and lemon. The house was glowing, with everything in its place. Lizzie and Charles had cleaned their rooms, and Lizzie had helped put clean sheets on all the beds, including the pullout couch in the den. Every closet and shelf was neat and tidy. There was even a bouquet of sweet-smelling yellow roses on the dining room table.

"I just want our house to look nice," Mom said every time Dad told her to take it easy. "The girls haven't been here in a long time."

Now, as they packed up the van, Mom piled another load into Lizzie's arms and handed Charles a dog bowl and a dog bed. "Don't forget Buddy's things," she said.

Buddy was already sitting in the van, ready to go. The little brown pup loved adventures, as long as they involved his favorite people. Each time Lizzie brought out a load, she petted him, rubbing the heart-shaped white spot on his chest. She loved Buddy so much, and she felt so lucky that he had found his way to her family.

The Petersons helped puppies who needed homes. They kept the dogs for only a short time, until they figured out the perfect home for each puppy. The hardest part of being a foster family was giving up the puppies when the time came—and in Buddy's case it had been impossible. The Petersons had agreed that he was part of their forever family, and he had come to stay.

Even Mom (who was more of a cat person, really) was crazy about Buddy. Still, Lizzie knew that she would be happy to have Buddy out of the house for the weekend. He was a good boy who never made messes or chewed things up, but after all, a puppy was a puppy. He might get excited with new people around. He might jump on her guests or try to run off with someone's shoe.

ABOUT THE AUTHOR

Ellen Miles loves dogs, which is why she has a great time writing the Puppy Place books. And guess what? She loves cats, too! (In fact, her very first pet was a beautiful tortoiseshell cat named Jenny.) That's why she came up with the Kitty Corner series. Ellen lives in Vermont and loves to be outdoors with her dog, Zipper, every day, walking, biking, skiing, or swimming, depending on the season. She also loves to read, cook, explore her beautiful state, play with dogs, and hang out with friends and family.

Visit Ellen at ellenmiles.net.